Bears Always Share

A Book About Manners

By Barbara Shook Hazen
Illustrated by Leonard Shortall

A GOLDEN BOOK • NEW YORK
Western Publishing Company, Inc., Racine, Wisconsin 53404

Library of Congress Cataloging-in-Publication Data

Hazen, Barbara Shook.
  Bears always share.

  Reprint. Originally published: Animal manners.
New York: Golden Press. 1974.
  Summary: In humorous verses, humanized animals deal
with a variety of social situations—some beautifully,
some rudely.
  1. Etiquette—Juvenile literature. [1. Etiquette]
I. Shortall, Leonard W., ill. II. Title.
BJ1857.C5H324 1986   395'.122   86-24563
ISBN: 0-307-15837-3
ISBN: 0-307-65837-6 (lib. bdg.)

Table of Contents

Bears Always Share

Bears share their toys,
Bears share their honey.
Bears share a joke
They think is funny.

Whatever they do,
Whatever they wear,
They share it with
Another bear.

Welcome, Ricky Raccoon!

When Ricky Raccoon comes over to play,
He helps put all of the toys away.
He asks his friend what he'd like to do
And always is careful with scissors and glue.

He washes before he comes to the table
And helps his host whenever he's able.
That's why almost every day
Someone invites Ricky over to play.

Watch Out for Wanda Warthog!

When Wanda Warthog comes over — beware!
She leaves a trail everywhere.
There's ink on the sofa, gum on the cat,
Modeling clay ground into the mat.

Her dirty fingerprints streak the wall.
She's broken her best friend's favorite doll.
Oops! There goes her dish of raspberry ice —
That's why poor Wanda is never asked twice.

11

Chimpanzees Ask
with a Please

Chimpanzees ask with a please.
"May I please"
Is what they say.
"May I please
Go out and play?"
"May I please
Borrow your bike?"
"May I please
Go on a hike?"
And when they ask
In such a nice way,
The answer is usually
"Yes. You may!"

Thank You, Gnu

The gracious gnu
Always says "Thank you."
Sometimes even better,
She says it in a letter.

Behave on the Bus, Rhinoceros

The rude and raucous
Rhinoceros
Shoves and pushes
To board the bus.

VN BUS CO.

He wiggles and jiggles
Around in his seat
And trips other folks
With his great big feet.

He sneezes and never
Covers his nose,
And everyone's glad
As soon as he goes.

15

Monkeys Climb All the Time

Little monkeys climb
Nearly all the time.
They climb on tables.
They climb on chairs.
They climb up clocks.
They climb down stairs.
They climb on the knobs
Of dresser drawers.
Why don't they ever
Climb outdoors?

16

Elephants Remember

Thoughtful elephants
Always remember
To wipe their muddy feet.
They come inside
When their feet are dried.
They're really very neat.

Don't Be Grabby, Gorilla

Gorillas are rude.
They grab their food.
They never say
"Please pass the peach."
They're so anxious

They just reach.
They upset others
By all they do.
And sometimes upset
The table, too.

18

Parakeet Chatter

Parakeets
Interrupt each other,
Father, sister,
Mother, brother.
"Chitter
Chatter
What's the matter?"
Everyone's chatter is so out of hand,
No one can hear
Or understand.
So if you want
To have your say,
Wait to speak.
It's better that way.

NORTH SOUTH

The Too-Loud Lion

When the lion roars
As loud as can be,
The monkey heads
For the nearest tree.

The elephant tries
To cover his ears.
The shy giraffe
Runs home in tears.
If he'd only speak
In a nicer way,
No one would want
To turn away.

Otters Are Thoughtful

Otters are thoughtful
In all they do.
They're always trying
To think of you.

When you're away,
They'll write you a letter.
When you're sick,
They'll make you feel better.

When you're thirsty,
They'll fill your cup.
When you're sad,
They'll cheer you up.

They'll lend you a sweater
Or make you a meal.
Thoughtful otters
Care how you feel.

23

Little Rabbits Have Good Habits

Young rabbits care
For their sisters and brothers.
They try to be good
To their fathers and mothers.

They are kind and fair
To friends and family.
That is how they
Live in harmony.

How Do You Do, Kangaroo?

When greeting grown-ups,
Joe Kangaroo
Puts out his hand
And says, "How do you do?"

And when they leave,
He doesn't forget
To smile and say,
"So glad we've met."

Greta Goat—
The Careless Kid

Greta Goat's a careless kid.
She loses everything.
Yesterday she lost her purse,
Now she's lost her ring.
How it happens or where they are
Greta never knows.
If she's lucky, maybe she'll find them
Under that pile of clothes.

"Just for You,"
Says the Kinkajou

"May I help you?"
Asks the kinkajou.
"May I take your bag?
May I tie your shoe?

May I push your wagon
Or pour your tea
Or help you with
Your ABC?
What pleases you
Is what pleases me.
Helpful is what
I like to be."

27

Rabbits at the Table

The rabbit twins always taste
The food that's on the table.
They don't always eat it all,
But they eat as much as they're able.
Funny, or runny, or something new,
They try at least a bite or two.

Not So Wild, Cats!

Wildcats make their mother roar
The way they slam the kitchen door.
If they would close it quietly,
They'd see how pleased their mom would be.

The Ox
Always Knocks

The ox always knocks
When he opens a door.
To barge right in
Makes some people sore.
Someone might be sleeping,
Or busy, or weeping.
Or, even more unpleasant,
Wrapping his present!
The ox always asks,
"May I come in?"
And everyone says,
"How thoughtful of him."

31

Seals on Wheels

Seals in trucks
And automobiles,
Seals on bikes,
All seals on wheels—
Are careful, considerate
Driver seals.

They look where they're going
And don't go too fast.
They toot their horns
If they want to pass.
And if there's someone
In the way,
''Please go first''
Is what they say.

Cut It Out, Coyotes!

When they play,
Coyotes fight.
They hit and kick
And sometimes bite.

Before the game
They play is done,
Someone gets hurt,
And no one has fun.

Pull Yourself Together, Pamela Pig

Pamela Pig
Is simply a mess.
Her hair's uncombed.
There's ink on her dress.
Her hands are filthy
And I have a hunch
That chocolate pudding
Was part of her lunch.
Doesn't she know
It isn't polite
To make others look
At such a sad sight?

The Too-Slow Sloth

Sammy Sloth
Is always last.
He never hurries—
Not even when asked.
No one can ever
Make Sammy move fast.

Never dressed
When it's time to go,
He misses the bus and
He misses the show.
Sammy's only speed
Is s l o w.

Terrible Tigers

Tiger cubs bicker
Night and day,
Day and night,
Whenever they play.
They bicker about
What they eat.
They bicker as they
Go to sleep.
Sister and brother
Scream at each other—
"You did it!"
"*I didn't!*"
"Yes, you did, too!"
"*No, I didn't!*"
"You know it was you!"
They bicker and battle
So constantly,
They drive their poor mother
Straight up a tree.

Leopards Look
Before They Leap

Leopards look before they leap,
They cross only with the light.
And when they cross
A crowded street,
They try to keep
To the right.

Smile, Crocodile

How sad, how sad is Claude Crocodile,
He never greets anyone with a smile.
His mood is always gloomy and gray,
No wonder his friends go the opposite way.

"Fair and Square," Says the Hare

"Play fair," says the Hare,
"In all that you do.
Take only the turn
That's coming to you.

"Never cheat.
Never sneak.
When playing cards,
Never peek.

"Don't run before
The count of three.
And if you lose,
Lose gracefully.

"Hey! Now I see you
Laughing and grinning.
I guess you played fair
And ended up winning!"

Be Glad You're You!

The leopard is proud
Of her spotted coat,
The nightingale
Of his song.
The elephant's glad
She has a trunk.
The lion's glad
He's strong.

They all agree,
"I'm glad I'm me.
No one's more fun
Or nicer to be."

44